The Monkey With No Bum

Written by Asa Murphy

Illustrated by Helen Poole

Murphy-World
Books

Charlie was a cheeky **monkey** who loved to have **fun!**
He was always playing and **jumping** around the house.
His mum and dad would often find him making **mischief!**

BECOME A MONSTER

Every day after school, Charlie would meet his monkey **friends** in the jungle for some fun and games before tea.

Those monkeys were full of energy and could really make some

noise!

Charlie's mum and dad loved watching the kids having fun through the window, but today, they noticed Charlie was **missing...**

"What's **wrong** Charlie?" asked his mum, when she found him on his bed. "Why aren't you outside with your friends?"

The Monkey Bum Parade!
2pm! All bums welcome!

"It's a very **special day** today, it's the **Monkey Bum Parade**, where all the monkeys show off their magnificent bums! It'll be such fun!"

But Charlie **didn't want** to join the Bum Parade.

He thought his **tiny, flat bum** wasn't worth wiggling.

Some of the meaner monkeys even called him 'The Monkey With No Bum' which made him feel sad.

The next day was a very **special** one for Charlie, it was his

birthday!

I don't know if you know this, but monkeys **love** birthdays! They have the best parties with music, lots of presents, jungle games and of course, **banana** birthday cake!

Charlie's mum and dad were especially excited this year as they had a **big** birthday surprise for him and **couldn't wait** to tell him!

When Charlie woke up that morning, he **jumped** out of bed, raced downstairs and shouted, **"Whoopee!** It's my **birthday!"**

After he'd opened his presents as fast as he could, his mum and dad gave him a **big** envelope.

"Here's something we hope will make this birthday **extra** special, Charlie."
The birthday boy ripped open the envelope and found a **gift card** for...

THE GREAT BIG BUM SHOP!

GIFT CARD

"**Yes! Yes! Yes!** Now I can have any bum I want! I can't believe it!" he squealed. "Thank you so much Mum and Dad, I'm going to choose the **biggest, fattest, reddest** bum and everyone will be jealous!"

"They won't be able to call me 'The Monkey With No Bum' then!"

That weekend, Charlie and his parents got the bus to **town** so he could choose his **new bum**.

The bus journey was fun and there was **SO** much to see on the way.

When they got off the bus, Charlie raced ahead.
"**Hurry up** slow coaches we don't want the bum shop to be **shut!**"

THE GREAT BIG BUM SHOP!

BUM BUNDLES!

BIG BUM BARGAINS!

BUMS IN ALL SIZES!

When he reached the shop, he thought it was the most **wonderful** sight he had ever seen.

OPEN

SALE

Charlie couldn't **believe** his eyes as he stepped inside.
There on the shelves was **every** type of monkey bum you could
imagine...

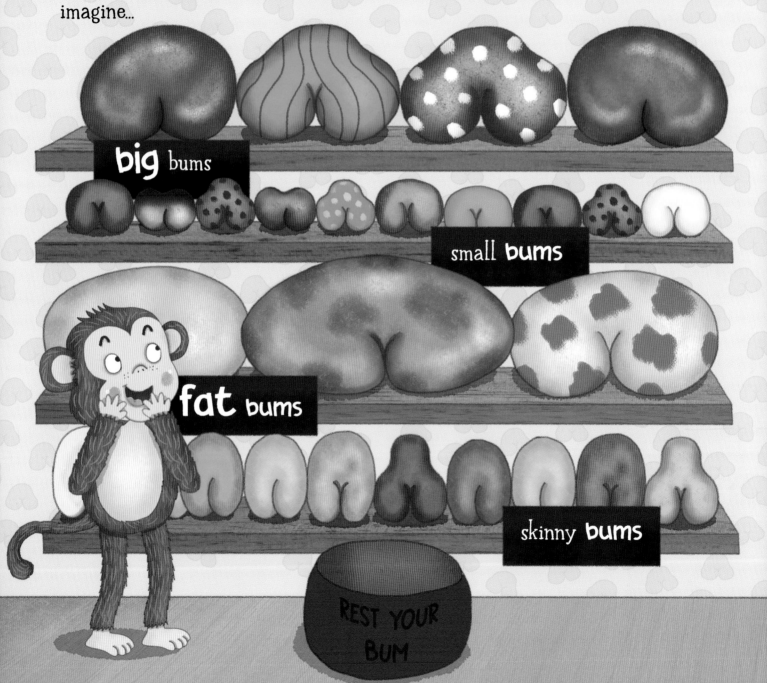

big bums

small **bums**

fat bums

skinny **bums**

REST YOUR BUM

hairy bums

red bums

green bums

yellow bums

There were even **spiky** and **bumpy** bums too!

REST YOUR

REST YOUR BUM

The shop assistant told Charlie to choose **any** bum he liked. He studied
the bums on the shelves and picked out the **biggest, reddest** bum
he could see.

Before Charlie went to try on his new bum, his mum and dad took him to one side. "We just want you to know how **proud** we are of you, Charlie, we love you and **every single thing** about you. We don't care if you have a big bum a red bum, a spotty bum or no bum at all."

"In our eyes, you're **perfect** just as you are."

Charlie took his new bum into the changing room and pulled the curtain shut.
After quite some time, he shouted, **"Ok, I'm ready."**

He pulled back the curtain to reveal his magnificent new bum...

"Ta-dah!"

Charlie smiled. He felt **lucky** to have such wise parents. "When I went into the changing room, I realised you were right. I **don't** need a great big fancy red bum to be liked. If people don't accept me as I am, then that's their problem, not mine."

"I'm **perfect** just the way I am, like we **all** are."

"In fact, I think I quite like having a **different** bum to the other monkeys!"

When Charlie got back from town, he **rushed** to the jungle to play with his friends.

"Hi Charlie! We've all **missed** you today! Join in with our game!"

Charlie played with his friends for hours. He had so much fun...

...and he wiggled his **perfect little bum** with pride.

In this world, we are all **special** and **unique.** If you ever worry about yourself in any way just remember Charlie...

'The Monkey With **Just The Right** Bum'.

Because like you, he was **perfect** in every way.

The End

Dedicated to my wife Kelly and children Shea and Poppy - Asa xxx
Dedicated to all my little monkey nieces and nephews - Helen xxx

Created in association with Robin Baynes MBE and Liverpool Heartbeat, inspiring young people in the North West of England to pursue healthy exciting fulfilled lifestyles since 2002.

First published by Murphy-World Books in 2020
Written by Asa Murphy
Illustrated, formatted and edited by Helen Poole
Text copyright © Asa Murphy
Illustrations copyright © Helen Poole

ISBN 978-1-8382971-0-7
Printed in the UK.

About the Author

After entertaining audiences for nearly 20 years as a singer songwriter, Asa Murphy has now turned his talents to writing a series of children's books containing valuable lessons for young people.

Website: www.asamurphyauthor.co.uk
Twitter: @AsaMurphy1
Facebook: Asa Murphy Self Penned

About the Illustrator

Helen Poole has illustrated over 200 books for publishers worldwide during her 12 year career and has also written and illustrated 4 rhyming picture books of her own. Her work has been featured on CBeebies Bedtime Stories and one of her books even popped up on Netflix series 'The Let Down'.

Website: www.helenpoole.com
Twitter/Facebook/Instagram:
@helenpoolebooks